A PRACTICAL GUIDE TO SOUL WINNING

Go Ye: The Call That Still Echoes

C. E. Pruitt and John F. Howell

DEDICATION

We are dedicating this book to a wonderful couple that helped make this book possible.
David and Linda Phillips
We love you both.

Foreword

In Matthew 28:18-20 is a Biblical admonition from the Lord Jesus Christ to His followers. It is called the Great Commission, and it is without a doubt the heartbeat of all true believers. It involves reaching the lost with God's plan of salvation found in Acts chapter two. It implies that the central mission of the Church is to find and save those that are spiritually lost. The Lord's assignment comes with a promise that He, Jesus will be with His followers as they go and obey His mission.

Since the obligation to reach the lost is for all believers, it is imperative and crucial that we be equipped for such a monumental task. John Howell and Charles Pruitt have given us a concise Scriptural declaration of the fundamentals of how to fulfill the mission Jesus called us to accomplish.

As you read and study this writing, I believe you will be inspired, encouraged, instructed and equipped to fulfill the assignment the Lord Jesus has given to each of us.

James E. Sandy

Table Of Contents

Welcome to The Practical Guide of Soul Winning

When we think of a world of over six billion people—each one a soul in need of God—the task before us can feel overwhelming. The need is so vast, the darkness so deep, that we can be tempted to shrink back, wondering how one life could ever make a difference. Yet the answer is not found in easier methods, quick schemes, or overnight successes that fade as fast as they appear. The answer lies in a timeless truth: reaching the world always begins by reaching one.

Instead of measuring ourselves against six billion, what if we simply looked across the fence at one neighbor? Instead of being paralyzed by the thought of millions in far-off lands like China, what if we turned to the one person whose path God has placed directly in ours? This was the method of Jesus. Though He spoke to multitudes, His heart always bent toward the one: a woman at a well, a ruler in the night, a fisherman by the sea. And it was the method of the early church. So powerful was their witness that their enemies declared: *"These that have turned the world upside down are come hither also"* (Acts 17:6).

The principle has not changed. The bricklayer does not build a wall in one motion—he lays one brick at a time. The timber jack does not fell a forest in a single swing—he cuts one tree at a time. And though the task is great, the "one-at-a-time" principle holds. I am reminded of the story of the timber jack who once interviewed for a job. When asked if he had cut much timber, he replied boldly, "Yes." "Where did this timber cutting take place?" they inquired. "In the Sahara Forest," he said proudly. "Don't you mean the Sahara Desert?" the interviewer asked. "Well," the timber jack answered, "it's the Sahara Desert now, but it was the Sahara Forest when I started cutting trees!"

This is what one person with a vision, with persistence, with a burning desire to reach a soul can do. The world is changed not in crowds, but in conversations. Not in sweeping movements, but in steady steps of faith. Not six billion at once, but one person at a time.

This book was not written with the group in mind—it was written for you, the one who will reach one more. It was written for the soul who dares to believe that their life, surrendered to God, can touch another life forever. Oh, what could just one individual do with a clear vision and a red-hot desire to reach just one soul?

When King Edward VII invited General William Booth, founder of the Salvation Army, to Buckingham Palace in 1904, he asked him to inscribe a few words in his autograph album. The seventy-five-year-old soldier of the cross bent forward, took the pen, and summed up his life's ambition in a few unforgettable lines:

Your Majesty,
Some men's ambition is art,
Some men's ambition is fame,
Some men's ambition is gold,
My ambition is the souls of men.

That is the ambition I long for in my own life, and the prayer I hold for yours. That when the sun sets on our earthly journey, we will not look back with regret. That we will have given ourselves, not to fleeting pursuits, but to what matters for eternity—the souls of men and women, reached one by one.

THE AUTHORS

Chapter 1

The Passion That Drives

Throughout this guide to soul winning, a golden thread will be woven—one that inspires us to be *that one* who reaches *one* for His kingdom. There is no higher calling, no greater joy, than to bring a soul from darkness into the marvelous light of Jesus Christ. Yet this sacred pursuit raises a question deep within our hearts:

How can we truly reach a soul destined for eternity—either to dwell forever in the mansion Jesus has prepared, or to be lost in a place of torment, separated from the presence of God?

Jesus Himself declared,

"For the Son of man is come to seek and to save that which was lost." *(Luke 19:10)*

And again He said,

"I am come that they might have life, and that they might have it more abundantly." *(John 10:10)*

He added this promise that steadies our hearts and fuels our mission:

"And I give unto them eternal life; and they shall never perish." *(John 10:28)*

"And if I go and prepare a place for you, I will come again, and receive you unto myself; that where I am, there ye may be also." *(John 14:3)*

The urgency of the hour could not be clearer. The mission remains the same. The call still echoes across generations—*Go ye into all the world.*

But how do we stay the course when the world around us is loud, demanding, and relentless? How do we, as stewards of the kingdom, guard our focus and keep from being entangled in the trivial distractions of life?

Scripture gives us the answer:

"Where there is no vision, the people perish." *(Proverbs 29:18)*

Focus

If we are to fulfill the call of God, we must renew our focus.

Setting right priorities, maintaining a clear vision, and staying consistent are essential to accomplishing anything of eternal value.

Daily prayer must be our anchor. Pray in the morning, pray in the evening, pray when the burden is heavy, and when joy fills the heart. *Pray always.*

"Pray without ceasing." *(1 Thessalonians 5:17)*

Prayer moves heaven. Prayer changes hearts. Prayer moves mountains. But most importantly—*prayer changes us.*

When we pray, God aligns our hearts with His. Our desires are reshaped until we begin to feel what He feels for lost souls. Oh, that we could see through His eyes and weep with His heart for those who wander without hope!

We Were Born to Be Soul Winners

With the infilling of the Holy Ghost comes not only power, but purpose.

"But ye shall receive power, after that the Holy Ghost is come upon you: and ye shall be witnesses unto me both in Jerusalem, and in all Judaea, and in Samaria, and unto the uttermost part of the earth." *(Acts 1:8)*

Your Jerusalem is your home, your family, your community. Your *Judaea* may be your workplace or city. Your Samaria might be those who are different from you. And the *uttermost parts of the earth* remind us that the gospel knows no boundaries.

Even Jesus testified,

"To this end was I born, and for this cause came I into the world, that I should bear witness unto the truth." *(John 18:37)*

As followers of Christ, the responsibility to reach the lost rests in the capable, Spirit-led hands of His Church—you and me.

Setting Priorities

To reach the lost, we must settle something deep within our hearts: *I am a soul winner.*

It's not merely an obligation or a ministry role—it's our identity.

This is what we were born to do.

If God be for us, who can be against us?

It is not His will that any should perish, but that all should come to repentance.

As Dallin H. Oaks once said, "Desires dictate our priorities, priorities shape our choices, and choices determine our actions."

What we love most determines where our energy flows. If our love for God and His mission comes first, everything else in life finds its rightful place.

When We Sow, We Will Reap

Jesus told a story that every believer should take to heart:

"A sower went out to sow his seed: and as he sowed, some fell by the way side; and it was trodden down, and the fowls of the air devoured it.

And some fell upon a rock; and as soon as it was sprung up, it withered away, because it lacked moisture.

And some fell among thorns; and the thorns sprang up with it, and choked it.

And other fell on good ground, and sprang up, and bare fruit an hundredfold." *(Luke 8:5–8)*

One plants, another waters, but God gives the increase.

The faithful farmer does not scatter seed carelessly. He prepares the soil with patience, tears, and trust.

"He that goeth forth and weepeth, bearing precious seed, shall doubtless come again with rejoicing, bringing his sheaves with him." *(Psalm 126:6)*

The seed is precious. The soil must be prepared. Passion for souls ensures that we *weep before we go*—because love moves us to labor.

Ezra Taft Benson wrote,

"When we put God first, all other things fall into their proper place or drop out of our lives."

Our love for God governs our time, our energy, and our focus.

Prayer Makes the Difference

Years ago, a dear brother shared a testimony that still stirs my heart. He had set out to reach his community, knocking on doors for hours, inviting families to church—but with little fruit.

Frustrated but not defeated, he made a new commitment: before he went to any door, he would first spend hours in prayer.

The results changed everything. Hearts opened. Families responded. Souls came to repentance.

The difference wasn't in the number of doors—it was in the time spent on his knees.

When we are sensitive to the leading of the Spirit, God will direct our steps just as He did for Philip:

"And the angel of the Lord spake unto Philip, saying, Arise, and go toward the south unto the way that goeth down from Jerusalem unto Gaza, which is desert." *(Acts 8:26)*

"Then the Spirit said unto Philip, Go near, and join thyself to this chariot." *(Acts 8:29)*

Through obedience, Philip met a searching soul—the Ethiopian eunuch—who would carry the gospel back to his homeland.

"And they went down both into the water, both Philip and the eunuch; and he baptized him." *(Acts 8:38)*

"And when they were come up out of the water, the Spirit of the Lord caught away Philip... and the eunuch went on his way rejoicing." *(Acts 8:39)*

What a picture of divine timing! Prayer positions us for encounters that only Heaven can arrange.

Who Prepares the Soil?

Jesus also gave a sobering parable about a barren tree:

"A certain man had a fig tree planted in his vineyard; and he came and sought fruit thereon, and found none." *(Luke 13:6)*

For three years, the owner sought fruit and found none.

"Cut it down; why cumbereth it the ground?" *(Luke 13:7)*

But the keeper of the vineyard pleaded,

"Lord, let it alone this year also, till I shall dig about it, and dung it: And if it bear fruit, well: and if not, then after that thou shalt cut it down." *(Luke 13:8–9)*

True passion for souls keeps us from giving up too soon. We dig, we water, we nurture—even when we see no fruit.

"And let us not be weary in well doing: for in due season we shall reap, if we faint not." *(Galatians 6:9)*

The bamboo lesson in Chapter Five reminds us: growth that begins unseen will one day break forth in strength. Faithful persistence always precedes a visible harvest.

The Potential of a Seed

Jesus compared the kingdom of heaven to something so small it could easily be overlooked:

"The kingdom of heaven is like to a grain of mustard seed, which a man took, and sowed in his field:

Which indeed is the least of all seeds: but when it is grown, it is the greatest among herbs, and becometh a tree, so that the birds of the air come and lodge in the branches thereof." *(Matthew 13:31–32)*

Even the smallest act of witness—a prayer whispered, a tract given, a conversation shared—can become a landmark of faith that blesses generations to come.

A single seed, planted in a willing heart, can become a tree that shelters a city—a beacon of grace that cannot be hidden.

One soul at a time. One story at a time. One act of compassion at a time.

Keys to Effectiveness

We can be effective in reaching the lost if we:

- **Stay focused** — Keep your eyes on eternity.
- **Be consistent** — Always sow, even when you don't see results.
- **Be willing to sacrifice** — Soul winning costs something, but the reward is eternal.
- **Be a good listener** — Listen not only with your ears, but with your heart.
- **Pray always** — Prayer prepares the soil and empowers the seed.
- **Love people** — Because love never fails.

The passion that drives us is not mere emotion—it is the heartbeat of God pulsing through His people.

When we align our priorities with His purpose, when prayer becomes our pattern and love becomes our language, then we can say with confidence:

"I am a soul winner."

This is who I am. This is what I was born to do.

Remember: If we go forth weeping, bearing precious seed, we shall doubtless return rejoicing—bringing our sheaves with us.

Chapter 2

What Is Your Spiritual I.Q.?

Proverbs 11:30 declares, *"...and he that winneth souls is wise."*

Everyone wants to be a winner. Whether it's a child around the kitchen table playing a game, an athlete training for the gold medal, or a hunter chasing the trophy buck, winning stirs something deep in us. But Scripture points us to a higher contest than games, trophies, or accolades. The wise winner is the one who wins souls.

If there is ever a pursuit worthy of our preparation, our focus, and our energy, it is this: to reach a lost soul with the message of Jesus Christ. Yet strangely, this is the very area that makes so many Christians uncomfortable. We'll sing off-key in front of others, we'll take on a class of rowdy children, we'll serve faithfully behind the scenes — but when the subject of soul winning comes up, our spirit tightens, our excuses begin, and our confidence collapses. Why?

The answer is simple. This is the front line of the battle between heaven and hell. Satan, the enemy of our souls, will do everything possible to keep believers silent and ineffective in this area. It is here that the eternal destinies of men and women are decided. It is here that our greatest calling meets our greatest resistance.

Statistics show that around 95% of church members have never personally won someone to Christ. Let that sink in. The greatest command we have been given — the Great Commission — is the one most often neglected. And yet Jesus said plainly, *"The harvest truly is great, but the labourers are few: pray ye therefore the Lord of the harvest, that he would send forth labourers into his harvest"* (Luke 10:2).

If we are to grasp the weight of this calling, we must first understand the value of a soul.

The Value of a Soul

Jesus asked, *"For what is a man profited, if he shall gain the whole world, and lose his own soul?"* (Matthew 16:26). In other words, put every diamond mine, oil field, skyscraper, farmland, and stock exchange into one pile. Stack it against one human soul. The soul outweighs it all.

Let's put this in perspective with real numbers found from Google research:

- **Gold:** By late 2024, all the gold ever mined on earth — about **212,582 tons** — was valued at over **$20 trillion**. Imagine owning every ounce of gold in every vault, jewelry store, and treasury. If you lose your soul, it profits you nothing.

- **Oil:** The world holds roughly **1.5 trillion barrels of proven oil reserves,** with several trillion more unproven. At market prices, oil wealth can be measured in the **hundreds of trillions of dollars,** shifting daily with demand and geopolitics. Yet Jesus said your soul is worth infinitely more.

- **Land & Real Estate:** Land itself cannot be priced in simple terms, but global real estate value was estimated at **$379.7 trillion** in 2022. And still, one soul is more valuable.

- **Stocks:** The combined value of all publicly traded stocks worldwide now exceeds **$120 trillion**, nearly half of it concentrated in the United States. But even if every market rallied in your favor, the Word of God says losing your soul would cancel out every gain.

Consider these staggering figures. Pile together gold, oil, real estate, and global stocks, and you approach wealth in **the hundreds of trillions — even quadrillions.** And yet, Scripture teaches that one solitary soul — yours, mine, your neighbor's, your child's — is worth more than all of it combined.

What is a man profited if he can catalogue the plants of the earth and yet never know the Rose of Sharon?

What is a man profited if he can chart the stars through a telescope but never meet Jesus, the Bright and Morning Star?

What is a man profited if he can study the ages of rocks but never know the Rock of Ages?

This truth is captured beautifully in the lines of an old hymn "If I Gained the World," written by Swedish hymn writer Anna Olander in 1904:

What will it profit, when life here is over,
Though gathering riches and fame,
If gaining the world I lost my own soul,
And in Heaven unknown is my name?

That question should stop us in our tracks. The soul is eternal. It cannot be measured by weight, currency, or time. It is the only possession that will outlast the grave. If you lose your soul, you lose everything. If you win Christ, you gain everything.

New Birth, New Mission

When we are born again, Scripture tells us we become "new creatures in Christ." But like natural infants, we begin as spiritual babies. A new believer should never feel embarrassed for not knowing every answer or for lacking eloquent speech. God does not expect polished sermons. He expects honest testimony.

Consider the Samaritan woman at the well. She did not rush back to town with a theological dissertation on "The Doctrine of Living Water." She simply said, *"Come, see a man"* (John 4:29). That invitation was enough to spark revival.

Or the blind man in John chapter 9. Jesus anointed his eyes with clay and told him to wash in the pool of Siloam. He obeyed and returned, seeing. Suddenly, the neighbors who had known him as a beggar were filled with questions: How did this happen? Who did it? Where is He?

The man's response was simple, straightforward, and powerful: *"A man that is called Jesus...I went and washed, and I received sight"* (John 9:11). He didn't have every theological answer. In fact, he didn't even fully know who Jesus was at that moment. But he had one undeniable truth: *"One thing I know, that whereas I was blind, now I see."* That was enough.

This is the heart of soul winning — not mastering every debate but bearing witness to the transformation Jesus has brought into your life. As we grow in Christ, we learn more. Just as children graduate from a bottle to a spoon, from a spoon to a fork, and finally to a knife, we grow in knowledge and maturity. But we do not wait until we are experts to share our story. We start where we are, with what we know:

the experience of grace.

Why Soul Winning Feels Hard

So why does soul winning still feel intimidating? Because it is spiritual warfare. Every soul is contested ground. Satan knows he is already defeated, but he fights tooth and nail for every life, hoping to blind, distract, and deceive.

But hear this clearly: you are not called to win souls in your own strength. The pressure is not on you to convert anyone. Your role is to be a witness. You are simply called to point people to Jesus, just as the woman at the well and the blind man did.

It is the Holy Ghost who convicts. It is the Word of God that transforms. It is Christ alone who saves. We are merely the messengers, the sowers of seed, the voices crying out, "Come and see."

Raising Your Spiritual I.Q.

If Proverbs 11:30 tells us that the one who wins souls is wise, then soul winning is not just about compassion — it is about spiritual intelligence. Your Spiritual I.Q. is not measured by how many verses you can quote or how many books you've read, but by your willingness to step into the harvest field and be used by God.

A high Spiritual I.Q. means:

- You recognize the eternal value of every person you meet.
- You understand that your testimony carries weight, no matter how simple.
- You see opportunities to plant seeds in everyday conversations.
- You overcome fear by relying on the Holy Spirit rather than yourself.

The greatest wisdom you can walk in is the wisdom that invests in eternity. Souls are the only treasures you can take with you into heaven.

A Call to Action

God has placed people in your path for a reason. Co-workers, neighbors, family members, the stranger you pass in the store — each one has an eternal soul of infinite worth. You may be the only light of Christ they will ever see.

You don't need to wait until you "know enough." If Christ has touched your life, you already have a testimony. Like the blind man, you can say, *"I was blind, but now I see."* That simple confession carries more power than you realize, because it is alive with the reality of God at work.

So let me ask you: What is your Spiritual I.Q.? Are you living with eternity in mind? Are you walking in wisdom by pursuing the greatest prize of all — the souls of men and women?

Today is the day to step forward. Start small but start. Pray for laborers — and then be willing to be the answer to that very prayer. Share your story. Invite someone to church. Extend a hand of kindness and let the Spirit open doors.

 Remember this: The only loss in life is a soul lost without Christ. The only true victory is a soul won for Him. And he that winneth souls is wise.

Chapter 3

THE BURDEN – THE NEED – THE SOUL

Isaiah 6:8 – *"Also I heard the voice of the Lord, saying, Whom shall I send, and who will go for us? Then said I, Here am I; send me."*

The Call and the Weight of Burden

There is always a weight to the call of God. The prophet Isaiah experienced it in a vision of the Lord, high and lifted up. His first response was not to volunteer but to confess his unworthiness. His lips were unclean, his people were unclean, and he knew he was inadequate. But after the cleansing coal touched his lips, the call came: *"Whom shall I send, and who will go for us?"*

It is the same today. God is still asking, still searching for those willing to carry His burden into the world. The call does not come to the qualified. It comes to the available. It comes to the one who dares to answer, *"Here am I; send me."*

In the Old Testament, the Levites understood this dynamic in a very literal way. They were entrusted with what Scripture calls "the service of the burden."

Numbers 4:47 – *"From thirty years old and upward even unto fifty years old, every one that came to do the service of the ministry, and the service of the burden in the tabernacle of the congregation."*

Think about that phrase: *"the service of the burden."* Ministry is not light. To serve God's purposes is to shoulder something weighty. The ark of the covenant was not carried on wheels but on shoulders. The tabernacle curtains, boards, and vessels were lifted by men who felt the weight of God's dwelling place.

In the same way, true New Testament ministry cannot be carried casually. It requires shoulders willing to bear the weight of souls. The question is not whether there is a burden—the question is whether we are willing to feel it.

Burdenless Religion

There is a danger in modern Christianity. We can have excellent services, professional music, eloquent preaching, polished programs— and yet no burden.

Yes, we should have "good church." There is nothing wrong with joy, excellence, and celebration. But if our joy never presses us beyond our walls into the highways and byways, then our joy has turned inward.

A burdenless church is a powerless church. A Christian without a burden is a Christian without alignment to God's heartbeat.

The early church did not grow because they had the best sound system or most comfortable seating. They grew because the burden of Christ burned in them like fire shut up in their bones. They could not remain silent. They prayed until they shook heaven, and heaven shook the earth.

We need that again. Not just energy, but earnestness. Not just songs, but supplication. Not just organization, but tears.

When Burden Shapes Prayer

When a real burden consumes us, prayer changes. Burdened prayer is different from casual prayer. It is not rushed, distracted, or shallow. It is travail. It is groaning too deep for words. It is Jacob wrestling until the break of day, unwilling to let go until blessing comes.

Ezekiel 47 speaks of waters issuing from the altar, flowing out and bringing life wherever they go. This is a picture of prayer. Revival waters flow not from pulpits first, but from altars. When we bend low, waters rise high. When tears fall, rivers flow.

This cycle is powerful. The more we pray, the more burden we feel. The more burden we feel, the more we pray. Far from draining us, this exchange fills us with holy strength.

And here is the mystery: the more we pour ourselves out in intercession, the more we are filled with the joy of the Lord. Burden does not crush—it compels.

Why Satan Fears Prayer

The late Samuel Chadwick once wrote:

"The one concern of the devil is to keep Christians from praying. He fears nothing from prayerless studies, prayerless work and prayerless religion. He laughs at our toil, mocks at our wisdom, but he trembles when we pray."

Hell does not tremble at our strategies, our intellect, or even our zeal. But when the weakest saint bends his knee in prayer, demons flee.

That is why prayer is attacked in your life. Notice how easy it is to scroll your phone, but how hard it is to sustain prayer. Notice how many distractions arrive the moment you decide to intercede. This is no accident—it is warfare.

The enemy knows: a praying church is a prevailing church. A burdened believer is a dangerous believer.

More Than Knowledge

George Sweeting, president of Moody Bible Institute, once shared a striking story. A woman came to him in distress:

"I have been a Christian for 20 years," she confessed. "I have memorized Scripture. I know how to answer objections. I know the right words to say. Yet I cannot name one soul I have led to Christ. Why has God not used me?"

Sweeting gently replied, *"Have you ever wept for the lost? Perhaps your struggle is not lack of knowledge, but lack of love. When you have compassion, you will weep over them, and you will yearn for their salvation."*

How true that is. We can fill our heads with theology, but if our hearts remain dry, our witness remains powerless. Knowledge informs us; burden moves us. And it is compassion that bridges the gap.

The Great Need

The need has never been greater than it is right now.

Our cities are full of people who know nothing of salvation. Some mask their emptiness with success. Others drown their pain with addiction. Many suffer silently with loneliness, depression, and hopelessness. They walk beside us in grocery stores, pass us on highways, and live in the houses next door.

And here we are—the light of the world, the salt of the earth. If we withhold the message, who will tell them?

Isaiah heard the voice of the Lord: *"Whom shall I send?"* That question echoes through history, and it is echoing still.

The Eternal Weight of the Soul

We must never forget: every person has a soul. Every cashier, every neighbor, every coworker, every child at the bus stop—each one has an eternal destiny.

This reality should shake us. Life is short. Eternity is long. And choices made in this brief vapor of time determine forever.

When we lose sight of eternity, urgency dies. But when eternity grips us, priorities shift. Suddenly, our schedules are not important and our comforts are trivial.

The burden is heavy, yes. To carry souls before God in prayer is to carry the very thing He values most.

Answering the Question

So, what will we do? Will we live comfortably within the walls of our churches, or will we say yes to the burden?

Isaiah's response was simple: *"Here am I; send me."*

This is the cry God longs to hear. Not excuses, not delay, not self-preservation—just surrender.

"Send me."

Send me into my neighborhood.
Send me into my workplace.

Send me to my family.

Send me to the stranger.

Send me into prayer until tears fall and lives change.

A Call to Action

Here is your challenge:

1. **Pray for a Burden** – Ask God to let you feel His heart. Linger until your heart breaks for what breaks His.
2. **Name the Lost** – Write down the names of people in your life who do not yet know Christ. Pray over them daily.
3. **Take One Step** – Speak, invite, or share your testimony. Begin small, but begin.
4. **Cultivate Compassion** – Refuse to grow numb. Ask God to give you tears for souls again.
5. **Answer Personally** – Don't pass the call to someone else. Be the one who says, *"Here am I; send me."*

Closing Appeal

The burden is not optional—it is the essence of the Gospel. The need is urgent—it is written on the faces of the people around you. The soul is eternal—it will outlast everything else in this world.

The Lord is still asking: *"Whom shall I send?"*

Let your answer rise today—not tomorrow, not next week, not "someday." Let your answer rise with the strength of surrender:

"Here am I. Send me."

African proverb: "There is only one crime worse than murder on the desert, and that is to know where the water is and not tell." We know where the water of life is!

🔥 **Tonight, before you close your eyes, set aside fifteen minutes. Kneel. Weep if you must. Pray for God to place His burden on your heart. Name the lost. Carry them to the altar. And tomorrow, step into your day ready to obey the Spirit's leading. The burden, the need, the soul—it all waits for your yes.**

Chapter 4

WHO IS MY NEIGHBOR? — WHERE IS MY WORLD?

Luke 10:29 – *"...who is my neighbour?"*

Mark 16:15 – *"And he said unto them, Go ye into all the world, and preach the gospel to every creature."*

Who Is My Neighbor?

A lawyer once came to Jesus with a loaded question. On the surface, it seemed innocent, even noble: *"Who is my neighbor?"* But Luke tells us the man's real intent: *"he, willing to justify himself..."* (Luke 10:29). His question wasn't born out of love for people—it was born out of self-preservation. He wanted the bare minimum requirements. He wanted to know: *"How little can I do and still be right with God?"*

Jesus didn't answer with a definition. He answered with a story. He told of a man beaten and left for dead on the road to Jericho. A priest came by—he saw the need, but passed by. A Levite came by—he too saw the man, but avoided him. Then came a Samaritan—despised, rejected, the last one anyone would expect to stop. Yet it was the Samaritan who poured in oil and wine, bandaged the wounds, put the man on his own beast, and paid for his care.

At the end of the parable, Jesus turned the lawyer's question around. The lawyer had asked, *"Who is my neighbor?"* But Jesus asked, *"Which of these three was a neighbor?"* The difference is subtle but life-changing. The lawyer wanted to know the boundaries of his responsibility. Jesus wanted him to see that *neighboring is not about labels—it is about action.*

Your neighbor is not determined by where they were born, what language they speak, what skin color they wear, or what political sign they post in their yard. Your neighbor is anyone you encounter who is in need—anyone God puts in your path.

Where Is My World?

In Mark 16:15 Jesus commanded, *"Go ye into all the world, and preach the gospel to every creature."* Matthew 28:19 says, *"Go ye therefore, and teach all nations..."* Acts 1:8 declares, *"Ye shall be witnesses... unto the uttermost part of the earth."*

The Bible is clear: the gospel is for **everyone**. No nation, no tribe, no neighborhood, no family is left out. But while the command is universal, the application begins right where we are.

Astronomers will tell you that we live on the third planet from the sun. From a scientific standpoint, our "world" is a ball of rock orbiting a star. But from a biblical standpoint, *your world is where you are.*

- Your world is your street.
- Your world is your workplace.
- Your world is your classroom.
- Your world is the grocery store line, the gas pump conversation, the late-night phone call from a hurting friend.

Before we can go to *the uttermost parts of the earth*, we must be faithful in Jerusalem. For you, "Jerusalem" may be your office cubicle. It may be your living room. It may be the neighborhood cookout, or the nursing home down the road. That is your world.

And here's the beautiful truth: if every believer reached their world, the whole world would be reached.

The Instinctive Desire of the Spirit

Judson Cornwall once wrote that the tragedy of modern life is that we are often consumed with the *"insistent demands of life"* while ignoring the *"instinctive desires of our spirits."*

Think about that. Instinctive desires are not forced. They are inborn, natural, and automatic. Birds don't attend flying school—they fly by instinct. Fish don't take swimming lessons—they swim by instinct. And for the Spirit-filled child of God, witnessing should be instinctive.

When the Holy Ghost fills us, the fire of God burns within us. Jeremiah described it as *"fire shut up in my bones."* He tried to keep silent, but he could not. His spirit compelled him to speak.

When God has truly touched your life—when you have tasted forgiveness, felt His presence, experienced His power—you don't have to manufacture a testimony. It should flow naturally, like a river springing out of the ground.

We talk about what excites us. A new parent cannot help but show pictures of their baby. A diehard sports fan cannot stop talking about their team's victory. A gardener cannot stop pointing out their roses. How much more should a redeemed soul speak of the One who saved them, healed them, delivered them, and promised them eternal life?

Witnessing is not a sales pitch. It is not memorizing a script. It is not knocking on a stranger's door with trembling hands. It is simply telling someone else the good news that has already changed your life. It is instinctive.

The Danger of Atrophy

But what happens when we suppress that instinct? What happens when we silence our testimony?

Just as unused muscles waste away, unused faith grows weak. Just as a neglected instrument goes out of tune, a neglected witness grows dull. When we hold back from speaking, we experience spiritual atrophy.

- Fruitfulness is never realized.
- Frustration begins to set in.
- Joy withers away.
- Doubt creeps in.
- And before long, the believer feels defeated, rejected, even useless.

The enemy delights in this. He doesn't have to make you a heretic. He doesn't have to lure you into blatant sin. If he can just keep you quiet—if he can just convince you to stay comfortable, stay safe, stay silent—then he has already won. You become another casualty, another statistic.

But it doesn't have to be this way.

The Samaritan Today

Imagine this: you are driving down the road, and you see someone stranded with a flat tire. Do you speed past, thinking, "I'm late, someone else will stop"? Or do you remember the Samaritan?

Picture a co-worker going through a divorce, sitting alone at lunch. Do you pretend not to notice, bury yourself in your phone? Or do you sit down and simply say, "I'm here if you need someone to talk to"?

Consider the cashier at the store who looks weary and burdened. Do you rush through, annoyed at the long line? Or do you take an extra moment to say, "I appreciate you. You're doing a good job"?

These may not seem like gospel sermons. But they are seeds. They are open doors. They are the beginnings of conversations that can lead to eternity.

Being a neighbor is not about doing everything—it is about doing something. And that something may be the very thing God uses to draw a soul to Himself.

No One Is Left Out

Jesus did not give this commission only to preachers. He didn't give it only to missionaries. He gave it to every believer.

- The preacher has a pulpit.
- The teacher has a classroom.
- The business owner has employees.
- The student has classmates.
- The stay-at-home parent has children and neighbors.

Every believer has a world. And every believer has a neighbor.

You don't need a passport to be a missionary. You don't need a degree to be a witness. You just need to be willing. *"Here am I, Lord— send me."*

A Stirring Call to Action

So, I ask you: Who is your neighbor? Where is your world?

Your neighbor may be sitting beside you right now. Your world may be the very place you've been praying to escape. But God has placed you there for a reason. He has positioned you as His ambassador.

This is not a burden—it is a privilege. This is not a chore—it is a joy. The God of the universe has entrusted you with the greatest message in history.

Don't bury it. Don't hide it. Don't let fear silence you.

Let the instinctive desires of the Spirit rise up within you. Speak when the Spirit nudges. Love when the Spirit compels. Act when the Spirit opens the door.

The world doesn't need more noise. It needs more neighbors. It doesn't need more arguments. It needs more love. It doesn't need more excuses. It needs more action.

You may never stand before thousands. You may never travel across oceans. But you can love your neighbor. You can reach your world. And if every believer did that, the world would be turned upside down.

So let us rise today with fresh courage. Let us throw off the chains of apathy, break free from the paralysis of fear, and walk boldly into our world with the gospel burning in our hearts.

For your world is waiting. Your neighbor is hurting. And the Spirit is saying, *"Whom shall I send, and who will go for us?"*

🜨 **May our answer echo the prophet's: "Here am I. Send me."**

Chapter 5

THE LAW OF THE HARVEST

John 4:35 – *"Say not ye, There are yet four months, and then cometh harvest? behold, I say unto you, Lift up your eyes, and look on the fields; for they are white already to harvest."*

There is a law written into the very fabric of creation. It is not man's law, nor is it subject to man's revisions. It is the eternal principle of God Himself. Farmers know it. Gardeners rely upon it. Nations rise and fall according to it. And the church is no exception. It is the **Law of the Harvest.**

The apostle Paul summarized it in Galatians 6:7: *"Be not deceived; God is not mocked: for whatsoever a man soweth, that shall he also reap."* This law is as sure as gravity, as unchanging as the sunrise, as binding as any promise of God. What you plant, you will harvest. What you neglect, you will lose. And what you faithfully water, God alone can cause to flourish beyond all measure.

Jesus told His disciples not to look to some distant future for the harvest, but to open their eyes and see that **the fields were already white unto harvest.** In other words, the time is not tomorrow—it is now. Souls are waiting. Lives are perishing. The wheat is white and ready to harvest...it's just waiting for laborers to reach out and gather it in.

But the harvest cannot come without sowing. And sowing cannot happen without labor. And labor will mean faith, perseverance, and trust that God will do what only He can do.

WE ARE EXPECTED TO PRODUCE

Jesus did not save us to sit idle. The Christian life is not a trophy case, where we dust off our salvation and admire it while doing nothing with it. It is a vineyard, a field, a garden in which God expects fruit.

In John 15, Jesus said, *"Herein is my Father glorified, that ye bear much fruit; so shall ye be my disciples."* Notice carefully: fruitfulness is not optional—it is the very evidence of discipleship. To bear nothing is to prove nothing. God expects His children to produce.

A barren branch is useless to the vine. It takes nourishment but gives nothing in return. So, Christ warns us of the fig tree, standing lush with leaves but bearing no fruit. When Jesus saw that tree, He cursed it—not because He hated trees, but because barrenness is a reproach. It is a mockery of purpose. A tree exists to produce fruit. A Christian exists to produce disciples.

GOD PATTERNED THE CHURCH AFTER THE FAMILY

In the Old Testament, the greatest heartache for a woman was barrenness. Rachel cried out, *"Give me children, or else I die!"* Hannah wept bitterly before the Lord, begging for the privilege of bearing life. Sarah, barren for so many years, received the miraculous promise of Isaac, proving that God's plan is always to bring life where there was none.

Barrenness was considered a reproach because it ran contrary to God's design. The family was meant to grow, to multiply, to bring forth children. In the same way, God patterned the church after the family. What happens in the natural is meant to mirror the spiritual. A healthy church should bring forth new children of faith. A healthy Christian should reproduce.

When a church ceases to win souls, it has forgotten its purpose. When a believer goes years without pointing someone to Christ, they have embraced a reproach. Just as a barren womb was a shame to the Old Testament family, so is a barren heart to the New Testament church.

OUR RESPONSIBILITY: TO PLANT AND WATER

But here is where we must be careful: fruitfulness does not mean forcing results. Our duty is not to engineer spiritual growth, but to faithfully obey. Paul wrote in 1 Corinthians 3:6: *"I have planted, Apollos watered; but God gave the increase."*

Do you hear the balance? Paul did what he could. Apollos did what he could. But the miracle belonged to God. You cannot save a soul—only Christ can. You cannot produce eternal life—only the Spirit can quicken. Your responsibility is to plant the Word, water it with prayer, and trust the Lord of the harvest.

Too often, we worry about what only God can do. We measure our "success" by how many visible results we can tally. But that is not our calling. Our calling is obedience. Our calling is faithfulness. Our calling is to keep sowing even when the ground looks barren, to keep watering even when nothing seems to break through the soil.

And that brings us to one of the most remarkable lessons from nature—the story of bamboo.

THE BAMBOO LESSON

Growing bamboo is not for the faint of heart. Especially in Malaysia, where the supreme grade of bamboo grows. Farmers there know that cultivating this precious plant takes patience, wisdom, and perseverance.

Author John Mason, in his book *"The Enemy Called Average"* wrote about growing bamboo.

Here is how it works:

- In the first year, you plant the seed. You water it faithfully. You fertilize carefully. You wait. And nothing happens. Not a sprout, not a leaf, not a whisper of growth.
- In the second year, you continue to water and fertilize. You labor with the same diligence, but again—nothing. Two years of work, and still no visible results.
- The third year arrives. Surely now something will break through? But no. Still nothing. You water. You fertilize. You labor. You hope. But the ground remains silent.
- The fourth year passes. The same routine. The same faithfulness. The same waiting. And still—nothing.

By now, many would have quit. Many would have plowed under the soil, assuming the seed had died. Many would have said, "This is wasted effort. I have labored in vain."

But the farmer who believes, who persists, who endures—he keeps watering. He keeps fertilizing. He keeps trusting.

Then comes the fifth year. And suddenly, without warning, the bamboo bursts forth from the ground. Not timidly. Not slowly. But explosively. It grows—are you ready?—**ninety feet in thirty to sixty days.**

From nothing to a nine-story building in such a short time. From barrenness to abundance. From silence to overwhelming harvest.

But here is the question: did the bamboo really grow ninety feet in thirty to sixty days? Or did it grow ninety feet in five years?

The truth is, the bamboo was growing all along. Its roots were spreading deep beneath the surface, establishing the foundation necessary to sustain such rapid growth. For four years, the real work was invisible. But when the time was right, the unseen became visible, the hidden became harvest, and the years of patient labor were rewarded in full.

THE SPIRITUAL APPLICATION

How often do we grow weary in sowing because we see no results? How many prayers have been abandoned in the fourth year, just before breakthrough? How many prodigals have been written off because nothing seemed to change? How many mission fields have been declared barren when the roots were just about to burst forth into life?

The bamboo teaches us this: **God's timetable is not ours.** Our part is to plant, water, and to labor faithfully. His part is the increase. **Just because you see nothing does not mean nothing is happening.**

Every prayer you pray is watering a seed. Every gospel conversation you share is planting truth in the soil of a soul. Every tear shed for the lost is fertilizing ground you cannot see. God is working in the hidden places, in the unseen roots, in the deep foundations of hearts.

And when the time is right—when His timing aligns with His plan—the harvest will come. And it will not trickle. It will burst forth.

THE HARVEST IS NOW

Jesus said, *"Say not ye, There are yet four months, and then cometh harvest?"* Don't look to the future. Don't say, "One day." Don't wait for the "perfect" conditions. He said, *"Lift up your eyes, and look on the fields; for they are white already to harvest."*

There are souls right now—your neighbor, your coworker, your classmate, your family member—ready to hear. Ready to believe. Ready to respond. The harvest is not some distant dream. The harvest is now. But it requires laborers. It requires sowers. It requires those willing to water through tears and endure through silence until God brings the increase.

A CALL TO ACTION

So, what must we do?

1. **Examine our fruitfulness.** Are we barren branches, or are we bearing fruit? Is our life marked by spiritual reproduction?
2. **Commit to sowing faithfully.** Plant the Word of God wherever you go. Conversations, prayers, tracts, invitations—every seed matters.
3. **Persevere in watering.** Don't quit in the second year. Don't despair in the fourth year. Keep praying. Keep fasting. Keep laboring. The roots are spreading even if you cannot see them.
4. **Trust God for the increase.** Lay aside the pressure to produce results. That is God's work, not yours. Your job is obedience.

His job is harvest.

5. **Lift up your eyes.** Look around. The fields are white. The harvest is now. Souls are waiting. Eternity is in the balance.

CONCLUSION

The Law of the Harvest cannot be broken. You reap what you sow. You reap after you sow. You reap more than you sow. The question is not whether the harvest will come—it is whether we will be faithful in the sowing.

Do not despise the days of small beginnings. Do not despair when nothing seems to be happening. The bamboo is growing, even if you cannot see it. The roots of revival are spreading, even if the surface looks barren. And when the time is right, God will bring forth the increase—sudden, overwhelming, undeniable.

So lift up your eyes, child of God. Look on the fields. The time for harvest is not tomorrow—it is today. The seeds are ready, the soil is prepared, the Spirit is moving. All that remains is for the laborers to rise up and say, like Isaiah of old, *"Here am I; send me."*

⬥ **Don't forget the law of the harvest. You will sow, you will water, and God—faithful, sovereign, eternal God—will give the increase.**

Chapter 6

METHODS OF APPROACH

Matthew 10:16 – *"Behold, I send you forth as sheep in the midst of wolves: be ye therefore wise as serpents, and harmless as doves."*

The Challenge of Approach

Jesus, in His great wisdom, did not hide the reality that reaching people with the gospel would not always be easy. He compared His disciples to sheep being sent into a world of wolves. That is not a picture of comfort, safety, or ease—it is a picture of danger, opposition, and resistance. Yet, in the same breath, He gave us the secret: *"be ye therefore wise as serpents, and harmless as doves."*

This is the balance of effective witnessing. Wisdom without gentleness becomes manipulation. Gentleness without wisdom becomes weakness. But when the two are combined—Spirit-led wisdom and Christlike meekness—the result is powerful, effective, Spirit-directed outreach.

This chapter is about **methods of approach**. Every believer has wondered at some point: *How do I begin the conversation? What do I say? Where do I start?* There is no single, rigid formula. There is no "one-size-fits-all" testimony. But there is a clear principle: your testimony must be **Christ-centered** and **Spirit-directed**. If Christ is at the center, and if the Spirit directs your words, your approach—whether simple or profound—will be used by God.

The Mandate of Compelling

Jesus told a parable of a great banquet in Luke 14. When the invited guests refused to come, the master of the house gave a startling command to his servant:

Luke 14:23 – *"And the Lord said unto the servant, Go out into the highways and hedges, and compel them to come in, that my house may be filled."*

Notice that word: *compel.* It means to urge, to press earnestly, to plead with sincerity and passion. This is not coercion. God never forces His love. Rather, it is persuasion. It is the heartfelt insistence that the invitation is real, urgent, and worth accepting.

Barnes' Notes comments on this verse:

"God in His infinite mercy invites the most wretched and vile man or woman to come unto Me, all ye that labour and are heavy laden, and I will give you rest. So, God in His great love toward us instructs his servants to compel or urge all to come."

Matthew Henry also adds:

"Go out into the highways and hedges... compel them to come in, but by force of arguments. Be earnest with them... convince them that the invitation is sincere and not a banter; they will be shy and modest, and will hardly believe that they shall be welcome, and therefore be importunate with them and do not leave them till you have prevailed with them."

This is the picture of evangelism: not casual, not halfhearted, not indifferent. But urgent, passionate, persistent. The gospel is life and death, heaven and hell, eternity itself. If we truly believe this, then our methods of approach must reflect a holy seriousness.

Where Do We Go?

The parable also answers the question of location. The master told the servant to go into both the **streets and lanes of the city** and the **highways and hedges.**

- **The Streets and Lanes of the City** – These could represent our immediate surroundings. The people closest to us. Neighbors. Coworkers. Friends. Family members. The people we see regularly at the grocery store, at school, and at the coffee shop. These are the ones who will "be glad to come," the ones who may be most open to an invitation.

- **The Highways and Hedges** – These could represent the overlooked, the marginalized, and even strangers. They may be the vagrants, the laborers, the hurting, the forgotten. They may not expect an invitation. They may doubt that they are welcome. But the Lord commands us to go to them as well. The gospel is not only for the easy-to-reach, but for the hard-to-reach.

The truth is this: **everywhere is the mission field**. Your world—your street, your workplace, your social circle—is your Jerusalem. Beyond that are your highways and hedges—the people you would not normally cross paths with unless you go out of your way. Both are necessary. Both are commanded.

Practical Methods of Approach

Now, let us consider some practical, Spirit-led ways to approach others with the gospel.

1. The Power of a Simple Invitation

Never underestimate the power of a warm, sincere invitation. "Would you come with me to church?" "Would you join me for a Bible study?" "Would you consider praying with me right now?" These may seem small, but God often uses simple invitations to open eternal doors. Andrew in the Bible didn't preach a sermon to his brother Peter—he simply said, *"We have found the Messiah... come and see."* (John 1:41–42). That simple invitation brought Peter to Jesus.

2. Connecting Through Current Events

Jesus Himself used the events of His day as bridges to spiritual truth. When people mentioned the tower of Siloam falling (Luke 13:4), He used it to speak about repentance. In our own conversations, mentioning world events—wars, disasters, cultural shifts—can create a natural bridge to talk about hope, peace, and the return of Christ. People are hungry for answers in uncertain times.

3. Asking Sincere Questions

A powerful way to open doors is simply to ask. "Do you have any kind of spiritual background?" "What has been your experience with God?" "Do you ever think about eternity?" Sincere questions not only show interest, they reveal where a person's heart is. And when someone shares their story, you can build on it with your testimony and the gospel.

4. One-on-One Bible Study

Perhaps one of the most effective approaches is sitting down with someone, Bible in hand, and letting the Word of God speak for itself.

Encourage them to use their own Bible. Let them read the verses aloud. Ask, "What does this verse say to you?" The Word of God is alive and powerful (Hebrews 4:12). When people see it with their own eyes, it penetrates deeper than any argument we could make.

The Uniqueness of You

Here is an encouraging truth: **God has given each of us a unique personality to reach people in a unique way**. Some are bold. Some are quiet. Some are analytical. Some are relational. Some can speak to crowds. Some connect best one-on-one. All are useful in God's hands.

The apostle Paul wrote:

1 Corinthians 9:22 – *"I am made all things to all men, that I might by all means save some."*

Paul adjusted his method without ever changing his message. He spoke differently to Jews than to Gentiles, to philosophers than to common laborers, to rulers than to prisoners. The message was always Christ, but the method varied.

In the same way, God does not ask you to become someone else. He asks you to be Spirit-led and authentic. Don't try to mimic another person's style. If you are naturally compassionate, let your compassion shine. If you are naturally bold, let your boldness be Spirit-controlled. The most effective witness is an authentic one.

The Call to Boldness and Love

There are two ditches in evangelism: fear and force. Some never witness because they are paralyzed by fear—fear of rejection, fear of awkwardness, fear of failure. Others approach with force—harsh words, argumentative spirit, pushing people away. But Jesus calls us to walk the middle path: **boldness with love.**

Boldness declares the truth without apology. Love delivers that truth with grace. One without the other is ineffective. Together, they are irresistible.

And remember this: success in witnessing is not measured by immediate results. Some will accept, some will reject. Our responsibility is not to convert hearts—that is God's work. Our responsibility is to plant seeds, to water faithfully, and to trust God for the increase (1 Corinthians 3:6).

A Personal Challenge

So, let me ask you: **Where will you go this week?** Who will you invite? Who will you compel? Whose name is God placing on your heart even now?

The streets and lanes of your city are waiting. The highways and hedges of your community are filled with people who may never know unless you go. The invitation is real. The house must be filled. The Master is still commanding, *"Go out... and compel them to come in."*

This is not a task for preachers alone. It is not a mission for missionaries only. It is the calling of every believer. You have been given a testimony. You have been filled with the Holy Ghost. You have been given your personality, your voice, your influence.

Now, go.
Go with wisdom.
Go with gentleness.
Go with urgency.
Go with love.

And as you go, remember this: you are not going alone. The same Christ who sent His disciples as sheep among wolves goes with you still. He has promised, *"Lo, I am with you alway, even unto the end of the world."* (Matthew 28:20).

Chapter 7

THE POWER OF ONE

Exodus 35:21

"And they came, every one whose heart stirred him up, and every one whom his spirit made willing . . ."

ONE LIFE CAN CHANGE EVERYTHING

The story of God's Word is not the story of multitudes moving as one mass, but rather of individuals—ordinary men, women, and children—who, when stirred by God's Spirit, dared to act. Again and again, history has been rewritten because **one life was surrendered to the will of God.**

God does not need a majority. He is not dependent upon numbers. He does not search for the rich, the powerful, or the influential. Instead, He looks for **one willing heart**—one person whose spirit is made willing, one soul stirred to obedience, one vessel that says, *"Here am I, Lord. Send me."*

- **David** was one boy with one sling and one stone, but in the hand of God, he became the deliverer of a nation.
- **A nameless lad** gave his one lunch, and Jesus multiplied it to feed thousands.
- **One widow**, down to her last meal, baked a cake for the prophet and opened the door to a miracle of supply.
- **Esther**, one woman, stepped into the king's court at the risk of

her life and saved her people from destruction.

- **Nehemiah,** one cupbearer, wept over the broken walls of Jerusalem and rebuilt a city.
- **Paul**, one man once blinded by sin, carried the gospel across nations and laid the foundation for the spread of Christianity.

Over and over again, God chooses to accomplish His greatest works through **one solitary individual** who dares to believe.

BUILDING OR WRECKING CREW?

"I watched them tearing a building down,
A gang of men in a busy town.

With a ho-heave-ho and lusty yell,
They swung a beam, and a sidewall fell.

I asked the foreman, "Are these men skilled,
The men you'd hire if you had to build?"
He gave me a laugh and said, "No indeed!
Just common labor is all I need.
I can easily wreck in a day or two
What builders have taken a year to do."

And I thought to myself as I went my way,
Which of these two roles have I tried to play?
Am I a builder who works with care,
Measuring life by the rule and square?
Am I shaping my deeds by a well-made plan,
Patiently doing the best I can?

Or am I a wrecker who walks the town,
Content with the labor of tearing down?"

This poem by Edgar Guest raises an important and serious question for all of us: "Am I a builder or a wrecker?"

Or what about the little poem, "Ten Little Christians" author unknown, has often been shared in church circles, and though it may make us smile, its truth cuts deep:

Ten church members came to worship all the time.
One fell out with the pastor, and that left nine.

Nine church members stayed up late,
One overslept, and now there are eight.

Eight church members on their way to heaven,
One took the broad road, and that left seven.

Seven church members all chirping like chicks,
One got offended at the music, and now there are six.

Six church members very much alive,
One got "travelitis," and now there are five.

Five church members all pulling for heaven's shore,
One got disgruntled over money, and this left four.

Four church members, all as busy as can be,
One got his feelings hurt, and now there are three.

Three church members, and the story is almost done,
Two grew weary, and this left one.

Now everyone knows there's not much one can do…
But one brought a friend last week—now there are two.

Two church members each won one more,
And don't you see? Two plus two equals four.

Four doubled to eight, who worked early and late.
Each brought another, and soon they were great.

In just a few weeks, through faithful pursuit,
That one had sparked a revival of 1,024!

The lesson is clear: **you are either in the building crew or the wrecking crew.** You are either multiplying or subtracting. Your one choice, your one word, your one attitude, makes a difference in the house of God.

ONE VOTE CAN CHANGE HISTORY

Even outside of spiritual life, the power of one is undeniable. Whole nations have been altered, governments reshaped, and destinies redirected—all because of a **single vote:**

- In **1839**, Marcus Morton became Governor of Massachusetts by **one vote.**
- In 1910, Charles B. Smith was elected to Congress from New

York by **one vote.**

- In **2017**, control of the Virginia House of Delegates came down to a single ballot—one vote determined which party would lead.
- In India in 2008, a national assembly election was decided by one vote out of over 120,000 cast.

Think of it: one citizen, one ballot, one decision—and history itself was rewritten.

If that is true in politics, how much more is it true in the eternal kingdom of God?

THE WORLD HAS YET TO SEE

Years ago, Henry Varley, a simple British preacher, spoke these words to a young Dwight L. Moody:

"The world has yet to see what God will do with a man fully consecrated to Him."

Moody heard those words, and they pierced his heart. He resolved, "By the grace of God, I will be that man."

The world is still waiting—not for committees, not for crowds, not for governments, not for systems—but for **one person totally on fire for God.**

THE VALUE OF THE "ORDINARY"

General Dwight Eisenhower once rebuked a fellow officer for belittling soldiers as "just privates." Eisenhower reminded him that the army could survive better without generals than without its privates. *"If this war is won,"* he declared, *"it will be won by privates."*

The church is no different. The gospel has always advanced on the shoulders of what the world calls "ordinary Christians." The ones who pray when no one sees. The ones who give when no one knows. The ones who faithfully serve in hidden places, raising their children, witnessing to neighbors, discipling one soul at a time.

God is not looking for the famous. He is looking for the faithful.

SATAN'S GREATEST FEAR

The enemy of your soul does not fear a great revival meeting nearly as much as he fears that you will catch a vision for the lost. He fears that you will wake up one morning and say, *"Enough! My life will count for God."*

Why? Because he knows what one soul on fire for Jesus can do. He knows the ripple effect of one prayer warrior, one faithful witness, one generous giver, one surrendered life.

It was one Luther who nailed 95 theses to a door and shook Europe.

It was one William Wilberforce who stood against the slave trade until it fell.

It was one Martin Luther King Jr. who raised his voice for justice and stirred a nation.

And it can be one you—if you will dare to believe.

THE CHALLENGE

So here is the question: Will you be the one?

- One prayer offered in faith can open the heavens.
- One act of kindness can soften a hardened heart.
- One invitation can lead a soul to Christ.

- One word of encouragement can save a brother or sister from giving up.
- One stone thrown in obedience can bring down a giant.
- One life, wholly consecrated, can alter eternity.

God is not asking if you are famous. He is asking if you are faithful. He is not looking for ability—He is looking for availability.

The power of one is not about the greatness of the vessel, but the greatness of the God who fills it.

A CALL TO ACTION

The Bible is filled with examples of individuals who rose up:

- Noah built one ark and saved a world.
- Joseph endured one prison and preserved a people.
- Moses lifted one staff and parted a sea.
- Joshua gave one shout and saw walls crumble.
- Rahab hung one scarlet cord and saved her family.
- Daniel opened one window and kept his prayer life.
- Stephen gave one testimony and opened heaven.
- Jesus prayed one prayer, died one death, and through His resurrection brought life to all.

You stand in that same line. You carry the same calling. You have the same God.

The Spirit is still stirring hearts. The question is: Will yours be one of them?

BE THE ONE

Never underestimate your life! Do not listen to the lie that says, "I am only one." For the truth is this:

- One candle dispels darkness.
- One seed brings a harvest.
- One drop creates ripples across an ocean.
- One cross saved the world.

The power of one in the hand of God is immeasurable.

So let the prayer of Isaiah be yours:
"Here am I; send me."

Let the cry of Moody be yours:
"By God's grace, I will be that one."

Let the testimony of heaven be written of your life:

This one made a difference. This one built the kingdom. This one obeyed God. This one mattered.

◊ **The world has yet to see what God will do through your one life, fully surrendered, wholly on fire for Him. Will you be the one?**

Chapter 8

Go Ye: The Call That Still Echoes

Mark 16:15 – *And he said unto them, Go ye into all the world, and preach the gospel to every creature.*

Matthew 28:19 – *Go ye therefore, and teach all nations.*

The final words of Jesus before His ascension were not suggestions—they were a divine command. He charged His followers with a mission that has echoed across centuries and continents: *Go ye.* Those two simple words carry eternal weight. They call every believer—not just the apostles, not only the preachers, but all who bear His name—to take the message of salvation into a world darkened by sin.

Christ did not send them unprepared. He gave them both the mission and the means. *"But ye shall receive power, after that the Holy Ghost is come upon you: and ye shall be witnesses unto me..."* (Acts 1:8). The Great Commission was never meant to rely on human strength, charisma, or ability. It was designed to flow through yielded vessels filled with the power of the Holy Ghost.

The apostle Paul understood this partnership when he wrote, *"We then, as workers together with him..."* (2 Corinthians 6:1). Soul winning is not our independent project—it is Christ working through us. When we go, we go in His authority, under His anointing, and with His abiding presence. The Lord does not send us alone; He goes with us every step of the way.

Understanding the Commission

To grasp the heart of this divine calling, we must understand what it means to be "commissioned."

The word *commission* is defined as "authority to act for, in behalf of, or in place of another."

The prefix co- means "together, in partnership," and mission means "a specific task with which a person or group is charged."

When Jesus gave the Great Commission, He extended His own mission to His Church. We were not called merely to attend church or maintain tradition—we were called to be **co-workers with Christ** in His redemptive plan.

Every Spirit-filled believer has been chosen, authorized, and empowered to represent the Gospel. The same Spirit that raised Christ from the dead lives in us to carry out His mission in the earth.

We are ambassadors of a heavenly kingdom, entrusted with the message of reconciliation. This is more than a duty—it is a privilege. He has called us, commissioned us, and equipped us. The entire world, from the crowded city to the quiet countryside, is our harvest field.

A Lesson from the Field

Years ago, my wife and I felt a burden for home missions. We began to pray about starting a church in a city that had no church of our faith. As I sought direction, the Lord impressed on my heart that His will is not always tied to a map—it is tied to a mission.

The will of God is not simply about where you stand, but who you reach.

Wherever there are souls in need, there is your field.

Wherever there is darkness, there is your calling.

Sometimes we wait for a perfect opportunity, a perfect location, or a perfect plan—but the Great Commission was never limited by circumstance. God's will is simply this: *that none should perish, but that all should come to repentance* (2 Peter 3:9).

When we obey the call to go, the Spirit of God begins to open doors, soften hearts, and make the impossible possible. The harvest belongs to Him; we are simply His laborers.

The Heart of the Shepherd

Jesus revealed the very heart of Heaven when He told the parable of the lost sheep:

Matthew 18:11–14

For the Son of man is come to save that which was lost.
How think ye? if a man have an hundred sheep, and one of them be gone astray, doth he not leave the ninety and nine, and goeth into the mountains, and seeketh that which is gone astray?
And if so be that he find it, verily I say unto you, he rejoiceth more of that sheep, than of the ninety and nine which went not astray.
Even so it is not the will of your Father which is in heaven, that one of these little ones should perish.

This is the compassion that fuels the Great Commission. Heaven rejoices over one sinner that repents. The ministry of reconciliation is not a burden—it's the heartbeat of God.

2 Corinthians 5:18 declares, *"And all things are of God, who hath reconciled us to himself by Jesus Christ, and hath given to us the ministry of reconciliation."*

We are not only saved from something—we are saved for something.

We have been enlisted to bring others to Jesus Christ.

The Lord's command still rings true: "Go out into the highways and hedges, and compel them to come in, that my house may be filled." (Luke 14:23)

Vision and Obedience

Eric Thomas once said, *"What you envision in your mind, how you see yourself, and how you envision the world around you is of great importance because those things become your focus."*

If you see yourself as a witness, your life will reflect it. If you see your workplace, your community, and your neighborhood as your mission field, you will begin to live intentionally.

Soul winning begins with vision—but vision alone is not enough. It must lead to obedience.

The Holy Ghost does not empower us for comfort; He empowers us for calling.

Albert Schweitzer said, *"If you love what you are doing, you will be successful."* When we love souls, when we love the work of God, we find fulfillment beyond measure. Success in God's kingdom is not counted in numbers but in obedience, faithfulness, and compassion.

The Psalmist captured it perfectly:

"They that sow in tears shall reap in joy. He that goeth forth and weepeth, bearing precious seed, shall doubtless come again with rejoicing, bringing his sheaves with him." **(Psalm 126:5–6)**

Every tear shed in prayer, every word spoken in faith, every tract given, and every testimony shared is precious seed. God promises that it will not return void.

The Excuse or the Call

Jim Rohn once said, *"If you really want to do something, you will find a way. If you don't, you'll find an excuse."* That truth echoes in the spiritual realm. The difference between a soul winner and a silent believer often comes down to willingness.

When compassion grows, excuses disappear.
When love deepens, fear diminishes.
When faith rises, hesitation fades.

Moses faced the same struggle when God called him to deliver Israel. He questioned his speech, his strength, and his suitability. Yet God assured him:

Exodus 33:14–15

And he said, My presence shall go with thee, and I will give thee rest. And he said unto him, If thy presence go not with me, carry us not up hence.

Like Moses, we can go forward with confidence, knowing His presence goes before us. The soul winner never walks alone.

God's Heart for the Lost

The Great Commission flows out of God's great compassion. The Lord is *"not willing that any should perish."* His heart beats for the lost.

The Gospel of Jesus Christ is the great light this dark world awaits. Isaiah prophesied,

"The people that walked in darkness have seen a great light." **(Isaiah 9:2)**

And still today, that light shines through us. We are called to reflect the glory of God in a world desperate for hope. Every conversation, every act of kindness, and every prayer sown for a lost soul is part of Heaven's redemptive plan.

The Urgency of the Hour

The need has never been greater. Our schools, communities, and even families are filled with those walking in darkness. The answer is not found in politics, programs, or policies—it's found in the power of the Gospel.

Isaiah's voice still challenges us:

Isaiah 62:1, 6

For Zion's sake will I not hold my peace, and for Jerusalem's sake I will not rest, until the righteousness thereof go forth as brightness, and the salvation thereof as a lamp that burneth.

I have set watchmen upon thy walls, O Jerusalem, which shall never hold their peace day nor night: ye that make mention of the LORD, keep not silence.

Now is not the time for silence. The world's noise grows louder, but the Church's message must rise higher. We carry the only hope that can save the soul.

Isaiah 62:11–12 declares:

Behold, the LORD hath proclaimed unto the end of the world, Say ye to the daughter of Zion, Behold, thy salvation cometh; behold, his reward is with him, and his work before him.

And they shall call them, The holy people, The redeemed of the LORD: and thou shalt be called, Sought out, A city not forsaken.

A Call That Still Echoes

Let it never be said that there was "no man." If you are reading these words, you are reading them by divine appointment. The harvest is now. The call is personal.

Jesus said, *"Lift up your eyes, and look on the fields; for they are white already to harvest."* **(John 4:35)**

The harvest does not wait for perfect timing—it waits for willing hearts. Souls are ready; Heaven is calling. Will you answer?

Isaiah saw a vision of a Redeemer who trod the winepress alone, saying, *"I looked, and there was none to help; and I wondered that there was none to uphold."* **(Isaiah 63:3–5)**

The price for redemption has already been paid. The cross is finished. But the message must still be carried.

Here Am I, Send Me

The same voice that called Isaiah still speaks:

"Whom shall I send, and who will go for us?" **(Isaiah 6:8)**

And the only answer that satisfies Heaven is: *"Here am I; send me."*

We are called, commissioned, and sent—not to build monuments, but to rescue souls. The Great Commission is not a burden but a blessing. To be chosen as a messenger of hope is the greatest honor a believer can receive.

Reflection and Call to Action

The time is short. The world is waiting. Heaven's call still rings clear: *Go ye into all the world.*

Let us not hesitate when eternity is at stake. Let us move with compassion, courage, and confidence in the power of the Holy Ghost.

If His presence goes with us—and it will—then no city is too hardened, no heart too distant, and no sinner too far gone.

For the fields are white. The hour is late. And the call still echoes: **Go Ye.**

🔥 **Remember: Let the Church arise. Let the light shine. Let every believer whisper, shout, and live these words:** ***"Here am I, Lord—send me."***

Chapter 9

The Heartbeat of Heaven

The Stirring That Will Not Rest

What causes an individual to wake in the stillness of night, heart burdened by a soul they met earlier that day? What compels someone to slip from a warm bed, fall to their knees, and weep—not for themselves, but for another's broken life? What unseen hand grips the heart so fiercely that one must rise and go, searching for that wayward one who has drifted from God?

This force is unlike any earthly ambition. It cannot be quenched by rejection or silenced by ridicule. The world cannot produce it, nor can the flesh sustain it. It is divine in origin—birthed in the very heart of God and planted within those who walk close to Him.

What is this fire that fuels the soul winner, ignites the preacher, and causes the saint to see the eternal instead of the temporary? The answer is one word—**Compassion.**

Compassion: The Heartbeat of God

Compassion is not soft pity or polite sympathy. It is not the sigh that says, *"I feel for you,"* yet remains unmoved. True compassion is love in motion—an inward stirring that cannot stand still.

The Hebrew word *racham* speaks of deep, motherlike affection. The Greek *splagchnizomai* means to be *moved from the inward parts.* When Scripture says Jesus was "moved with compassion," it describes a holy surge of divine love—a pull so strong that action becomes inevitable.

Compassion moves. Compassion acts. Compassion pays the price. It is the bridge between seeing and doing. Without it, the needs of the lost are noticed but never met. With it, mountains are climbed, oceans are crossed, and souls are saved.

The Compassion of Christ

Every act of Jesus' ministry flowed from compassion:

- **When He saw the sick, He healed them.**
  "And Jesus went forth, and saw a great multitude, and was moved with compassion toward them, and he healed their sick." — Matthew 14:14
- **When He saw the hungry, He fed them.**
  "I have compassion on the multitude, because they continue with me now three days, and have nothing to eat." — Mark 8:2
- **When He saw the weary crowds, He taught them.**
  "He was moved with compassion on them, because they fainted, and were scattered abroad, as sheep having no shepherd." — Matthew 9:36
- **When He came to Lazarus' tomb, He wept.**
  "Jesus wept." — John 11:35
- **When He beheld Jerusalem,** knowing its judgment, He wept again.
  "And when he was come near, he beheld the city, and wept over it." — Luke 19:41

Jesus did not minister out of obligation. He ministered out of love—love that wept, healed, and reached. His compassion changed everything it touched.

Compassion That Makes the Difference

Jude wrote, *"And of some have compassion, making a difference."* — Jude 22

Indeed, compassion makes the difference—the difference between duty and delight, between walking by and stopping to help.

In the parable of the Good Samaritan (Luke 10:30–37), a wounded man lay half-dead on the road. The priest passed by. The Levite passed by. Both perhaps pitied him—but neither acted. Then came a Samaritan, despised and rejected, who was *moved with compassion.* He bound the wounds, carried the man, and paid the cost.

The priest had religion. The Levite had position. But only the Samaritan had compassion. And only compassion made a difference.

David once cried, *"I looked on my right hand, and beheld, but there was no man that would know me: refuge failed me; no man cared for my soul."* — Psalm 142:4

May that never be said of us—that we passed by without caring for the soul of another.

Compassion Beyond Appearances

Compassion looks beyond the surface. It sees past dirt and scars, tattoos and tears. It does not stop to assign blame. It simply loves.

But compassion also peers past the polish of success. The businessman, the celebrity, the politician—all can hide empty hearts behind a smile. Money may buy pleasure but never peace; comfort but never contentment. Only Christ can satisfy the longing soul.

And only compassion will look beyond appearances and reach for the heart within.

The Driving Force of the Soul Winner

Skill, eloquence, or strategy alone cannot win a soul. Without compassion, our words fall flat and our efforts fade. But when compassion burns, even halting speech is anointed by the Spirit.

Paul expressed it in Romans 9: *"I have great heaviness and continual sorrow in my heart... For I could wish that myself were accursed from Christ for my brethren."*

Such love is not natural—it is supernatural. Jeremiah called it "a fire shut up in my bones" (Jeremiah 20:9). Compassion is a burden that refuses to rest until action is taken.

Modern Expressions of Compassion

Consider the missionary who leaves home and family to reach distant shores.

Consider the pastor who prays through the night for wandering sheep.

Consider the believer who gently shares Christ with a hurting co-worker.

Each act springs from the same source—**compassion.**

It is the driving force that keeps us knocking on one more door, praying one more prayer, shedding one more tear, and extending one more hand.

The Call to Compassion

There will always be broken, wounded souls in life's ditches. There will always be someone whispering, "No man cares for my soul." The question is—will we care?

When General William Booth, founder of the Salvation Army, could no longer attend his convention, he sent a single-word telegram: **"Others."**

That one word captures the heartbeat of Heaven.

Others—that is compassion.

Others—that is the fire that moves the soul.

Conclusion: The Strength of Divine Love

Compassion is not weakness—it is strength wrapped in mercy. It is not optional—it is essential. It is the difference between barren effort and fruitful ministry.

May the Lord fill our hearts with this divine fire—to weep over the lost, to act in mercy, and to never pass by a soul in need.

For when compassion grips the heart, the driving force of Heaven moves the hands and feet of man.

"And of some have compassion, making a difference." — Jude 22

May it be said of us that we cared.
May it be said of us that we acted.
May it be said of us that our lives were driven—not by pride, not by fear, not by duty—but by **compassion.**

(Hymn by Charles D. Meigs written in 1902)

OTHERS, LORD, YES OTHERS

Lord, help me live from day to day
In such a self-forgetful way
That even when I kneel to pray
My prayer shall be for others.

OTHERS, LORD, YES OTHERS,
LET THIS MY MOTTO BE,
HELP ME TO LIVE FOR OTHERS
THAT I MAY LIVE LIKE THEE.

Help me in all the work I do
To ever be sincere and true
And know that all I'd do for You
Must needs be done for others.

Let self be crucified and slain
And buried deep: and all in vain
May efforts be to rise again,
Unless to live for others.

🔥 **Remember: The Heartbeat of God is…OTHERS!**

Chapter 10

LAST THOUGHTS

Revelation 22:20 – *"He which testifieth these things saith, Surely I come quickly. Amen. Even so, come, Lord Jesus."*

The Wisdom of Winning Souls

Proverbs 11:30 declares: "The fruit of the righteous is a tree of life; and he that winneth souls is wise."

But what would be its opposite? If soul winning is wisdom, then soul neglect is folly. If the fruit of the righteous is life, then the barrenness of silence is death. If obedience to the Great Commission is wise, then indifference is sin.

There is no neutral ground in eternity. We are either standing with Christ in His mission—or standing in neglect against Him. We are either wise soul winners or foolish deserters of our duty.

War and the Will to Fight

History has always known the cost of conflict. General William Tecumseh Sherman summed it in three words: "War is hell." Carl von Clausewitz, the shy but brilliant Prussian strategist, wrote, "War is the continuation of politics by other means." Yet beneath their definitions, one principle stands: war is ultimately decided by will.

Nations have lost battles, though they had the greater weapons. Armies have triumphed though they were outnumbered. Why?

Because one side possessed a will that refused to yield.

If this principle holds true in earthly war, how much more in spiritual war? We wrestle not against flesh and blood, but against principalities, powers, and rulers of darkness (Ephesians 6:12). Souls are at stake. Eternity is on the line. Victory will not go to the most eloquent, nor the most resourced, but to the ones who will not quit.

O God, grant us the **will** to fight for the souls of men. The resolve to go into the flames, the determination to carry the gospel to the ends of the earth, the courage to stand at our post until the trumpet sounds.

Into the Fire – The Houston Tragedy

On May 31, 2013, a five-alarm blaze consumed the Southwest Inn in Houston, Texas. Four firefighters lost their lives, and fourteen were injured.

The tragedy revealed more than flames—it revealed the nature of the place itself. The inn, once called the Roadrunner, was notorious for drugs, prostitution, violence, and crime. Behind a cheap coat of paint and a new name, a black-market world thrived.

When the fire struck, a friend of mine, Mickey Blagg, asked a Houston fire captain, "How is it that four of the bravest and best of HFD rushed into a burning inferno to rescue the dregs of society?"

The captain's answer was unforgettable:

"We are not trained to judge... we are trained to save lives."

Did you hear it? Do you get it? The firefighters of Houston, trained to save temporal lives, risked everything without hesitation. They did not stop to ask if the victims were worthy. They did not pause to evaluate their lifestyle. Their duty was simple: **go in and save.**

And yet, we who hold the only message that saves men eternally too often hesitate. We judge. We weigh. We excuse ourselves. All while the flames of sin and hell consume lives around us.

If four firefighters could give their lives to save men from temporary flames, how can we not give ours to save men from eternal ones?

The Witness of the Faithful

Through history, God has raised up men and women who understood this call:

- **David Brainerd** – consumptive with tuberculosis, coughing blood as he preached to Native Americans, dying at twenty-nine. Yet his journal still stirs passion centuries later.
- **William Booth,** founder of the Salvation Army, thundered: *"Go for souls, and go for the worst!"* He built an army that marched into the alleys, brothels, and prisons of England.
- **Jim Elliot,** martyred on the riverbanks of Ecuador, wrote before his death: *"He is no fool who gives what he cannot keep to gain what he cannot lose."* His blood became seed for a missionary movement that carried the gospel to nations.
- **Hudson Taylor,** who left comfort to penetrate the heart of China, once said, *"The Great Commission is not an option to be considered; it is a command to be obeyed."*

None of these measured the cost—they had already surrendered it. None of these judged the worthiness of the lost—they knew the worth of the cross.

The Question of Eternity

Beloved, the lines are drawn. The hour is late. The prize is eternal. The trumpet is already at the lips of the angel. Christ is coming quickly.

So where are the laborers?
Where are the intercessors?
Where are the soul winners?
The Scripture does not say, *"He that buildeth great businesses is wise."*
Nor, *"He that gathereth wealth is wise."*

But only this: **"He that winneth souls is wise."**

Every day, 150,000 people step into eternity. Every second, two souls leave this earth forever. Hell enlarges itself, but heaven awaits those who will go.

On that day when we stand before the throne, titles will not matter. Degrees will not matter. Bank accounts will vanish. Our comfort, our excuses, our delays will be gone. Only one question will remain:

Who did you bring with you?

The time for hesitation is over. The trumpet is about to sound. The King is on His way.

A Final Prayer – The Altar Call of this Book

O Lord, break my heart for what breaks Yours.
Set eternity before my eyes.
Burn away my apathy, my excuses, my fear.
Give me tears for the lost, courage for the fight, and a voice
that will not be silent.

Make me a rescuer, not a spectator.
Make me a soul winner, not a soul neglecter.
Make me wise with the wisdom of heaven.

Here am I, Lord.
Send me.
Use me.
Spend me.
Until the trumpet sounds and I see Your face.

Even so, come, Lord Jesus.
Amen

www.ingramcontent.com/pod-product-compliance
Lightning Source LLC
Chambersburg PA
CBHW071441300726
48976CB00004B/1408